FOR CHIHIRO — P. P.

FOR OLIVIA GRACE — M. B.

FOR OLIVIA AND SAKAI — R. D.

Book design by Kristen M. Nobles.
Typeset in Mramor and House of Death.
The illustrations for this book were rendered in pen and ink and acrylic
on Fabriano 300-pound coldpress watercolor paper.
Manufactured in China.

Library of Congress Cataloging-in-Publication Data
Pollack, Pam.
Halloween night on Shivermore Street / by Pam Pollack & Meg Belviso; illustrated by Randy DuBurke.
p. cm.
Summary: The Halloween party on Shivermore Street is not to be missed, especially when the clock strikes thirteen.
ISBN 0-8118-3946-X
[1. Halloween–Fiction. 2. Parties–Fiction. 3. Stories in rhyme.]
I. Belviso, Meg. II. DuBurke, Randy, ill. III. Title.
PZ8.3.P5593 Hal 2003
[E]–dc21
2002013238

Distributed in Canada by Raincoast Books
9050 Shaughnessy Street
Vancouver, British Columbia V6P 6E5

10 9 8 7 6 5 4 3 2 1

Chronicle Books LLC
85 Second Street
San Francisco, California 94105

www.chroniclekids.com

HALLOWEEN NIGHT
ON SHIVERMORE STREET

I'm thirsty!

By Pam Pollack and Meg Belviso * Illustrated by Randy DuBurke

chronicle books · san francisco

There's a party tonight on Shivermore Street—
a fancy-dress, masquerade ball!

The moon's pea green. It's Halloween.
Come, put on your masks, one and all.

Trick-or-treating down Shivermore Street
to the house at the end of the block.
Approach if you dare—
beware the loose stair—
and give the old door a loud knock.

The hinges creak. It opens wide.
It's **SIX O'CLOCK**—step right inside.

There's a truckload to eat on Shivermore Street:
sizzling spiders hot out of the pan,
fresh fly-trapping plants,
whipped-cream-covered ants.
Come gobble as much as you can.

We eat until we're really stuffed—
by **SEVEN O'CLOCK** we've had enough!

There are musical chairs on Shivermore Street.
Six witches, five chairs, music stops.
A race for the seat,
a tangle of feet,
and down on the floor one witch plops.

No more chairs—a final shout.
By **EIGHT O'CLOCK** last witch is out.

Five vampires are carving on Shivermore Stre

five pumpkins set out in a row.

Everyone races

to cut pumpkin faces.

Five candles set them aglow.

Jack-o'-lanterns burning bright—
at **NINE O'CLOCK** they're quite a sight!

We're bobbing for apples on Shivermore Street.
The werewolves are lining up now.
Though they've got great big teeth
above and beneath,
they still miss the apples somehow.

Werewolves stomp off, stomachs growling.
By **TEN O'CLOCK** they're really howling.

We're hiding and seeking on Shivermore Street.
One fat little ghost is tagged It.
He counts up to ten,
turns around once and then—
watch out! If you're caught he might spit!

We run to home base one by one.
By **ELEVEN O'CLOCK**
the game is done.

It's time for the limbo on Shivermore Street.
Four mummies have brought out a broom.
They bend way down low,
then under they go,
trailing wrappings all over the room.

Mummies get a tight re-rolling.
Now the **MIDNIGHT** hour is tolling.

We're do-si-do-ing on Shivermore Street.
The goblins and ghouls skip and jump.
They stamp and they bite.
Promenade to the right.
Now back to back, everyone bump!

The moon's pea green. It's Halloween—
and time for the clock to strike…

THIRTEEN?!

In the Halloween house on Shivermore Street
we all hold our breath as it strikes.
Everyone in your place?
Now—take off your face!

Ready, set,

ONE,

TWO,

THREE,